~ Also by Caridad Piñeiro ~

Current Releases as Charity Pineiro

NOW AND ALWAYS June 2013 ISBN 1490362770
FAITH IN YOU July 2013 ISBN 1490412697
TORI GOT LUCKY December 2013 ISBN 1494775182
THE PERFECT MIX March 2014 1495948234
TO CATCH HER MAN April 2013 ASIN B00JJ7RK1C

Current Releases as Caridad Pineiro

Books in The Gambling for Love Romantic Suspense Series

THE PRINCE'S GAMBLE November 2012 ISBN 9781622668007 Entangled Publishing
TO CATCH A PRINCESS August 2013 ISBN 9781622661329 Entangled Publishing

Books in THE CALLING/THE REBORN Vampire Novel Series

VAMPIRE REBORN, March 2014, ASIN B00J3GHA3C
DIE FOR LOVE, December 2013, ASIN B00H6EFD5U Entangled Publishing
BORN TO LOVE, November 2013, ISBN 9781622663705 Entangled Publishing
TO LOVE OR SERVE, October 2013, ISBN 9781622663477Entangled Publishing
FOR LOVE OR VENGEANCE September 2013 ISBN 9781622662937 Entangled Publishing
KISSED BY A VAMPIRE (formerly ARDOR CALLS) October 2012 ISBN 9780373885589 Harlequin Nocturne

Books in The Sin Hunter Paranormal Romance Series

THE CLAIMED May 2012 ISBN 978-0446584609 Forever Grand Central Publishing
THE LOST August 2011 ISBN 978-0446584616 Forever Grand Central Publishing

JUST ONE NIGHT

Caridad Pineiro

He has just one night to prove to her that anything is possible . . .

Jason Hart, Jase to his friends, has just graduated college and earned his commission as a Second Lieutenant in the Marine Corps. It's the night of the graduation party and she'll be there. His best friend's slightly older sister, Nickie. Nickie is the only woman he's really wanted for a long time. He has just one night to make it happen.

She has just one night before the man of her dreams leaves, maybe forever, but can she find the courage to take a chance . . .

Nicole de Salvo has been in love – and lust – for her little brother's best friend for years. For years she's watched from afar and done nothing about her attraction for Jason Hart only now their time together is almost at an end. On their last night together will she find the courage to do something about her feelings, or will she live with regret for the rest of her life?

Sale of this book without a front cover may be unauthorized. If this book is coverless, it may have been reported to the publisher as "unsold or destroyed" and neither the author nor the publisher may have received payment for it.

This book is a work of fiction. Names, characters, places, and incidents are the product of the author's imagination or are used fictitiously. Any resemblance to actual events, locales, or persons, living or dead, is coincidental.

Copyright © 2014 by Caridad Piñeiro Scordato

All rights reserved. Except for use in any review, the reproduction or utilization of this work in whole or in part in any form by any electronic, mechanical or other means, now known or hereafter invented, including xerography, photocopying and recording, or in any information storage or retrieval system, is forbidden without the written permission of Caridad Piñeiro Scordato.

All rights reserved under International and Pan-American Copyright Conventions. By payment of the required fees, you have been granted the non-exclusive, non-transferable right to access and read the text of this e-book on-screen. No part of this text may be reproduced, transmitted, down-loaded, decompiled, reverse engineered, or stored in or introduced into any information storage and retrieval system, in any form or by any means, whether electronic or mechanical, now known or hereinafter invented, without the express written permission of publisher.

Visit Caridad's website at www.caridad.com.
JUST ONE NIGHT Cover design ©2014 Kim Killion
Manufactured in the United States of America

To my wonderful daughter, Samantha, my best friend forever.
You rock and I am totally proud of you.

Chapter 1

Nicole de Salvo stared out the train window as every passing mile brought her closer to home . . . and to him.

It had been a hectic day with a dash down to the Philadelphia area for her brother's and Jase's graduation and then a rushed trip back to New York City for an interview for a position she wanted for her summer break from medical school. An interview that couldn't be rescheduled no matter what.

The nearly two hour train ride down to her family's home on the Jersey Shore was long, but at least it would give her a moment to catch her breath and prepare for seeing him again.

For seeing Jase, possibly for the last time.

He had looked amazing that morning in his dress uniform, sword at his side and his second lieutenant's bars gleaming in the morning sun. The deep blue of the uniform had made his green eyes seem aqua, like the ocean bathed with brilliant light. Tall and imposing, he had looked every inch an officer and a warrior until he had fixed his gaze on her and offered up the wicked little boy grin that did all kinds of things to her insides.

She pressed a hand to her stomach to quiet the nervous flutters as she thought about seeing him again once she arrived at home, where her younger brother Tommy's graduation party would be in full swing. It had been tough enough seeing Jase that morning, knowing that with every minute that passed their time together was fading away.

This night at the party and knowing it would be the last one they'd share was going to be one of the hardest things she ever did.

Driving that thought from her mind, she glanced out the train windows and caught glimpses of the shoreline and ocean visible from the North Jersey Coast line.

They'd all spent so much time in those waters, her, Tommy, and his best friend Jason. Jase to his friends.

She was a friend, kind of. After all, they'd grown up together and had spent many a lazy summer along the shore. But as they'd gotten older, something had changed.

The typical teasing between kids, between her and Jase, had become more flirty. Definitely full of subtle sexiness. Or at least, it had gotten that way on his part.

She hadn't known how to handle it when an eighteen year old Jase had settled that green-eyed gaze on her, flashed her a not-so-innocent dimpled grin, and heat had ignited inside her. Four years later, she still didn't know how to handle him.

He was like a little brother to her, although the annoying voice in her head shouted a big, "Hell to the no" and reminded her that they were only two years apart in age.

Reluctantly she admitted to herself that Jase was definitely *not* like a little brother. Not since she'd come to understand that the weird little tingle she got whenever she saw him or talked to him meant that there was way more to her feelings for him.

More that she had yet to explore, only time was running out for them.

As the train chugged along on her way home, she dragged up the memory of what he'd looked like as he'd sauntered up to her this morning after graduation, looking every inch the hero. His swimmer's shoulders looking even broader in his uniform. His green eyes bright and warming as they settled on her. His smile had been inviting as he'd leaned in and kissed her. Chastely, but she'd wanted to linger and have it be more. She had wanted to savor those amazing lips before she had reined herself in. She reminded herself that she never would give in to that desire because she was too sensible and responsible and downright boring.

She closed her eyes to hold in the memories. Allowed herself to imagine what it might be like to be with Jase. To let go and explore the temptation.

In her mind's eye, she pulled his white dress hat off his head and tossed it to the side. Skimmed her fingers through the buzz cut sandy-colored hair at the sides of his head and the longer strands up top before cradling his head and drawing him near for a not so simple kiss.

She covered his mouth with hers and pulled at his bottom lip with her teeth, urging him to open for her. When he did, she dipped her tongue in and tasted him. Trailed her tongue all around and nipped at the fullness of his lips with her teeth.

His strong hands were at her waist, holding her close. Possessively hard and yet gentle as he dragged her closer, but she shifted away because she wanted more than just his kiss.

She trailed her hands down to his shoulders and then lower to his lean waist and the shiny brass buckle with the Marine insignia. As she undid the buckle and loosened his white belt, he snared his sword as the belt started to drop, and gently laid them both on the ground.

"Are you sure about this?" her dream Jase asked as he rose to stand before her again.

"Oh, yeah, I'm sure," her imaginary self answered because her real self lacked the courage to take a chance with Jase.

He helped her open the brass buttons down the front of his dress blues, and in her fantasy, his chest was bare beneath the wool fabric.

His skin was a luscious honey gold thanks to his end-of-summer tan. He got that smooth golden color from being a lifeguard on the beach to earn money for college and other necessities.

How many times had she snuck a peek at him up in the stand as she'd sat under her umbrella, reading her latest romance novel?

Not that you needed a sexy fictional alpha hero when you had your own just feet away if only you'd do something about it, the little voice in her head had screamed more than once during those long lazy summers.

She forced away the annoying voice and resumed her fantasy, running her hands down across the chiseled muscles of that tanned chest. His skin was sun-kissed warm and slightly damp. She needed a taste and leaned forward, licked from the center of his chest to the hard masculine nipple that she sucked, earning a soft moan from him. He tasted salty like the ocean.

She smiled and moved her hands down toward his waistband, and he helped her by undoing his pants and letting them drop.

He had gone commando (this was her fantasy after all) and his cock was rock hard. Long, thick, and smooth beneath her hand as she encircled him.

He groaned and his eyes fluttered close as he said, "I like that, Nickie."

"I like, too, Jase," she said and kept on stroking the length of him. Loving the heat of him beneath her hand and how his cock swelled at her caress of the sensitive head.

When he opened his eyes again, they were dark, almost emerald-colored with his desire. He leaned forward and kissed her and as the kiss grew more intense, she opened her mouth and accepted the slide of his tongue. Imagined him easing his dick inside of her the way he was making love to her with his mouth and tongue.

She sucked in a shaky breath and circled her index finger around the head of his cock where the first hint of his release wet the tip. She spread it all over, earning a rough growl from him that vibrated through her body. Her clit throbbed and swelled and between her legs, she grew wet for him.

"I want to be in you, Nickie. Now," he whispered against her lips.

"Now," she repeated and urgently tore her clothes away as he sank down to the blanket spread out on the sand and lay there, waiting for her. Gloriously naked with his beautiful cock standing at attention for her.

He held his hand out in invitation, a hesitant look on his face, not that he needed to worry. In this daydream, she wouldn't refuse his request.

She took hold of his hand and lowered herself until she was straddling his thighs. She poised above him and his hands gripped her hips hard and slowly urged her down onto him.

Friction built as each thick inch of him filled her. She relished the heat and pressure as she pushed down until he was completely buried inside her. She stilled and gazed at him. Felt immense power and sexiness as his eyes drifted closed again and his head dropped back in pleasure.

"You feel amazing, Nickie. So hot and wet. Tight, fuck me, you're so tight."

Leaning down, she splayed her hands on his chest and stroked her thumbs across his hard masculine nipples, dragging his eyes open.

"You're amazing, Jase. The way you fill me. The way you make me feel. Touch me, Jase. I want your hands on me," she said, not hesitant in her dreams about what she needed from him. About what she had fantasized about for so long during those lazy summer days and even longer nights as she'd laid in bed, achy and hot for him.

He grinned, displaying the dimple that made him look so much younger. She skimmed her finger across that cute indent and he speedily turned his head and nipped her index finger with his perfect white teeth.

"I'd rather taste you," he said and before she could protest, he surged up and put his mouth on her breasts, sucking and biting at the sensitive tips.

His mouth was heaven and she cradled his head to her and offered up soft cries of enjoyment, but soon she couldn't just stay there with him buried inside her. She had to move. Had to satisfy the need created by the magic of his mouth on her breasts.

She lifted her hips, the friction of the motion intense. Even more so as she drove back down quickly and ground her hips against him.

His rough groans spurred her to move again and again until her actions were wild and the sound of their bodies slapping together filled the air together with their guttural moans of pleasure.

Inside her the tension built, ever higher until her release shot through her and she arched her back and pushed down on him hard, her clit and pussy throbbing and vibrating with the pleasure of her release.

"Jase," she said softly beneath her breath.

"Miss? Miss! We're at Long Branch. Time to change over to the Bayhead train," the conductor said, a hint of irritation in his voice.

Startled, she sucked in a rough inhalation as reality rudely intruded and warmth flooded across her cheeks as if she had just been discovered butt naked on the train, but she hid her embarrassment.

She offered up an apologetic smile, rose, and hopped off onto the platform. For a moment she considered that it would be far safer to get on the next train back to New York City. But she forced herself to cross the platform to the diesel train waiting there for the next leg of her trip. Forced herself to get on board the train.

It was finally time to face both her past and her future.

It was long past time to face Jase.

Chapter 2

Nicole slipped out of the taxi she had grabbed at the train station and hurried into her family's beachside home. She was able to sneak in through the front door without being noticed since most people at the party were either outside or in the immense great room at the back of the house.

Dragging her suitcase upstairs, she hurried to her bedroom. She was already so late for the party that she had decided during the cab ride not to waste time and change out of her interview suit, but then she caught sight of herself in the mirror.

Her dark, nearly black hair was scraped back from her face into a serviceable topknot that made her face look severe and way too serious. The bright white of the shirt and dark grey of the suit were extremely professional and definitely not party wear.

Boring, the little voice in her head complained, but she ignored it.

Their guests would understand that she'd just hurried home from New York City and hadn't had time to change.

Do you really want to look like someone's Old Maid aunt? the annoying voice in her head shouted and as she glanced at the mirror again and grimaced at what she saw, it was way to hard to ignore that voice.

Do I? Do I want to look like this when it could be the last night I see Jase for a long long time? she asked herself.

For all her life, she'd played it safe. She'd been the good little girl who did everything that her parents asked. Straight A student. Never broke curfew. Never did anything that would make someone raise an eyebrow in surprise.

It was why she'd never done anything about her attraction to Jase. Well, at least nothing anyone would know about. In the quiet of her room during those long summer nights, she'd definitely done lots to satisfy the need that Jase had made her feel.

But maybe tonight was about doing something different. Maybe tonight was about doing something that no one would expect.

Not even Jase.

With that thought in mind, she marched to her walk-in closet and searched through the racks of clothes her mother had bought for her and which just collected dust for the most part. The words Nickie and fashionista were never used together.

She flipped through outfit after outfit until her gaze settled on the bright crimson dress and the matching three inch stiletto heels just beneath it.

It was the kind of dress that said, "Look at me."

As for the stilettos, her girlfriends would call them "Fuck me shoes."

Her hands shook as she grabbed the dress and shoes, hoping he would look. Hoping he would possibly do more.

As she dressed, hesitation set in again, but she pushed it back and walked toward the mirror, but she still wasn't satisfied with what she saw.

There was just one more thing to do. She undid the clips holding her hair back, shook her head and her cascaded onto her shoulders. Suddenly a different woman stood there, gazing back at her from the mirror.

A sexy and confident woman. One who would know what to do with Jase.

She prayed that she wasn't about to make the worst mistake of her life.

* * *

Jason Hart mingled through the crowd, sipping his celebratory glass of champagne.

Not that he felt much like celebrating, although he should.

Today had been a monumental day in his life.

He had graduated from college, the first in his family to do so. And since being commissioned, he was now officially an officer in the United States Marine Corps.

Oohrah. I should be happy, he thought and took another sip, but he'd been nursing the bubbly for so long that it was warm and had gone slightly flat. It was a lot like the flatness he was feeling about his life right now since despite all his achievements, he had no one really special to share them with.

Across the way, his parents were chatting with some neighbors attending his best friend Tommy's graduation party. His graduation as well, but his parents were planning a much smaller and less luxurious party in their new North Carolina home. Like so many Jersey folk, they'd fled harsh winters and even harsher taxes for an easier life.

A few feet away, Tommy and his parents mingled with their guests.

His family and Tommy's were special to him, but as he scoped out the area, he acknowledged that the one really special person who would have made it feel different was missing.

Shoving away thoughts of Nickie because it would only bring disappointment on a day that should be filled with joy, he mingled with the guests attending the party.

It was a day to celebrate and he wasn't going to let Nickie's absence ruin the joyful mood of the night.

She'd show up eventually and they'd say hello and act as if there was nothing going on between them.

There wasn't, not really. For years and years and years, he'd been attracted to his best friend's older sister. Only he hadn't really done anything about that other than tease her a little.

Okay, maybe he'd teased her a lot, not that she'd ever seem to notice or do anything about it which had made him back off to avoid coming off as a stalker kind of guy.

As a waiter passed by, he exchanged his warm flat glass of champagne for a fresh one. Sipped it as he mingled and waited for the one person who could make this the special kind of night it should be.

He waited for Nickie.

* * *

Jase Hart stood out from the crowd gathered down below much like he always did, Nickie thought.

He was dressed in his Marine uniform, looking oh so beautiful and handsome. Much like she had pictured him during the fantasy on her long train ride home.

He'd taken off his white dress hat and it was tucked under one arm, exposing his sandy blond hair. In the summer months, the sun would streak those strands with brightness, giving him that perfect surfer look. Especially when combined with those wide shoulders that tapered down into lean hips.

His amazing eyes, looking a little more blue than green thanks to the color of his dress uniform, were alert and focused on the man before him. At something the man said, Jase smiled, displaying that boyish dimple on one side of his all too tempting mouth.

All she had to do was walk down the stairs and over to him. It was such a short distance away physically, but despite her earlier thoughts and bravado, it occurred to her that Jase was untouchable for way too many reasons.

He was her younger brother's best friend.

He would soon be gone and risking his life.

He would never ever never be interested in a woman like her. A woman who couldn't seem to make up her mind about what to do about him. A woman who lacked the strength to reach for what she wanted most.

Jase needed a strong woman by his side. One who could man the home front while he was off to war. One who wouldn't be indecisive or wimpy.

You only have one night left. Take a chance, said the voice of the dreamer that she repressed way too often.

With those conflicting thoughts rattling through her head, she sucked in a deep breath, tossed her shoulders back, and walked down the stairs.

* * *

Jason caught sight of Nicole de Silva as she glided down the sweeping staircase in an eye-catching red dress that hugged every enticing curve of her body. The color set off the creamy color of her skin and dark as midnight hair that spilled down across her bare shoulders, thick and with a life of its own as she moved.

More than once he had imagined tunneling his hands into that hair and pulling her close. Kissing her until she was clinging to him and he could take her to bed and do what he'd wanted to do to her for way too long. As his gaze drifted down her long lean legs and to the enticing red stiletto heels, he imagined dragging them off her feet as he kissed his way up her body.

"So where did you say you were deploying?" the man beside him repeated, pulling him away from thoughts of Nickie.

Nickie was off limits, he reminded himself. The Bro Code demanded that he had to keep his hands off even though he itched to run them all along that fabulous body and have those incredible legs wrapped around him as he made love to her.

"Afghanistan," he finally answered, but then his attention to the man fled as he realized Nickie was walking his way. "Would you excuse me for a moment?" he said, sidestepped the man and hurried toward her.

He met her halfway across the crowded great room in her family's home.

They stood there awkwardly for several hesitant heartbeats, staring at each other. With the high heels, she was almost eye level with him and her mouth was just inches away. Her luscious mouth done in an enticing red that dared him to lean in and kiss her.

But instead he just stood there, not really sure where to begin. Anxious about what to say and where it might lead. Feeling like a total fool for being so indecisive. The only thing that offered him any relief was that she was obviously as unsure of what to do as he was.

She nervously played with the small black clutch in her hand before hesitantly saying, "Congratulations, Jase. It must be very exciting to be done with school and earn your commission."

"Thank you, Nickie. I hear you're doing well. How's medical school?" He dragged his gaze away from her hands and to the soft swell of her breasts visible above the neckline of the body-hugging dress before meeting her gaze. Her eyes were a gorgeous light hazel color with flecks of chocolate brown and hints of gold.

"Good, thanks. I'm enjoying the challenge," she replied, looked away from him and glanced around uneasily. "I really should mingle, you know. I've already missed too much of the party because I had that interview in New York."

Disappointment slammed into him, but he hid it. He was a fuckin' Marine for God's sake and he wasn't going to let her see just how much he wanted that she spend some time with him before he left.

"Sure, Nickie. I guess I'll see you later," he replied.

She turned and started to walk away, but then she stopped and faced him again.

"I'm going to miss you, Jase," she said and then rushed off.

I'm going to miss you, too. A lot, he thought.

Feeling the need for something stronger to wash away the sense of defeat that had filled him, he marched to the bar and ordered a bourbon. The bartender poured him the drink and he was about to step away when Tommy sauntered up and clapped him on the back.

"What's your poison, dude?" Tommy asked and shot a quick look at his glass.

"Bourbon," he answered and his friend jerked his chin in the bartender's direction.

"Can you pour me one as well? Thanks," he said and the man quickly placed the drink in front of him.

Tommy snared the tumbler and clinked it against his. "To the blue and white," Tommy said, referring to their alma mater's colors.

He smiled and raised his glass, "To the blue and white." After a bracing sip, he stayed beside his best friend, but his mind was on Nickie as she stood across the room, chatting with an older couple. She shot a quick look his way, smiled hesitantly, but then turned her attention back to the guests.

"How long have we known each other, Jase?" Tommy asked as he jammed one hand in his suit pocket and took a sip of the drink in his other hand.

He shrugged and said, "Since kindergarten when we were on the same T-ball team."

"That's a long time to be friends," Tommy said thoughtfully, but then plowed on. "In all that time, I've never seen you be afraid of anything. Well, maybe *one* thing."

He peered at his friend and searched out his features, puzzled by his statement. "Where are you going with this, Tommy?"

His friend raised his index finger off the glass he held. "You've got one night, Jase. One night before you head to North Carolina with your parents and then ship out to that fuckin' desert."

"It's actually not a desert, Tommy," he said, trying to avoid the discussion he sensed was coming, but Tommy was apparently not going to stop.

"Dude, don't be a fucktard. Don't you think it's time you did something about my sister?" he said.

Jase nearly choked on the bourbon he had been sipping and stared hard at his friend. "You're fucking crazy."

"No, I'm not. But you are if you don't do something about it."

"It" being Nickie. "You're really serious about this, aren't you?"

"I am, Jase. I know you care for her. I've known for a while. I also know you've never let anything stop you before. What's stopping you now, bro?"

Tommy's gaze was so intense, that he had to look away, not wanting his friend to see what he was really feeling. He shook his head hesitantly. "I'm the last thing she wants. We're nothing alike. She's so serious and a bookworm. And I'm – "

"All action guy. Not as wealthy as us. Those are lame excuses, dude. I guess you feel guilty because she's my sister, too. But you know what, Jase? It's time to do something about what you feel for Nickie. It's time to go big or go home. Just don't hurt her," Tommy pleaded and before Jason could say another word, his friend clapped him on the back again and hurried off to where his parents stood with some friends.

Go big or go home.

How many times had they said that to each other on the playing field? Too many times to count.

But Nickie wasn't a game to be played. Nickie was special to him and had been for some time. Nickie was everything he could ever want in a woman. She was bright and beautiful. Caring and honorable. Incredibly sexy, not that she seemed to know that.

And he'd just gotten the green light to go for it from his best friend. From a man he thought of as a brother. *Her* brother.

Slugging back the last sips of his bourbon, he took a deep breath and rushed toward her. He had only this one night to make it happen.

He wasn't going to waste another minute. After all, a Marine never backed down from even an impossible task.

Not even an incredible and seemingly unattainable challenge like Nickie.

Chapter 3

From the corner of her eye, Nickie caught a glimpse of her brother stalking from the bar at the far edge of the great room and of Jase who stayed rooted there, looking her way. His square-cut jaw was tense and his lips were in a firm line. Dimple-less. His gaze was so . . . intense.

A second later, Jase was marching in her direction, purpose in every long and powerful stride.

He was clearly a man on a mission and her heart sped up at the thought that she might be his intended target.

"You must be very proud of your brother," said the older gentleman across from her. He was a business associate of her father's and she forced her attention back to him, smiled and nodded.

"We are proud of him and I know Dad is very excited that Tommy will be joining him in the family business."

"He's going for an MBA, isn't he?" the man's wife asked just as Jase reached them.

"Yes, yes he is," she said, but stumbled with her next words as Jase laid a possessive hand at the small of her back. "H-h-a-ave you met Lieutenant Hart? He's an old family friend."

"Thank you for your service, Lieutenant Hart," the man said and Jason dipped his head gratefully.

"Thank you, sir. I hope you don't mind if I steal Nicole away for a little bit."

Before she could protest, he exerted gentle pressure at her back and urged her away from the couple and toward the French doors leading outside.

"What do you think you're doing?" she hissed beneath her breath and plastered a smile on her face, trying not to attract too much attention as he hurried them out the doors and to the large flagstone terrace that ran along the back of the house.

It was a beautiful early summer night and many of their guests were gathered outside to enjoy the weather. Various tables and chairs had been laid out on the terrace and at the far end, a second bar had been set up to serve drinks to the party-goers. Luckily most people were gathered in that area as Jase led them toward the edge of the terrace.

"You and I need to talk," he said and urged her to the lawn beyond the flagstone, but she dug in her three inch heels and skidded to a stop.

He faced her, a determined look on his features. He shifted his hand to her waist and held her possessively. His touch punched the air from her lungs and awakened sharp need as she imagined him urging her closer and closer until . . .

"What do you think you're doing?" she repeated to stop those too sexy thoughts.

He glanced all around the terrace and his lips thinned into a grim line again. He leaned near and whispered in her ear, "Not here, Nickie. Please come with me somewhere private."

He moved his hand away from her waist and slipped it into hers, twining his fingers with hers as if afraid she'd pull away. He tugged gently, prodding her to follow him as he turned and strode toward the beachfront.

It was crazy to go, she thought, but it was just as crazy not to explore where this night might take them.

* * *

Jase breathed a sigh of relief as Nickie relented and followed him down the steps of the terrace and onto the lawn. He waited for her as she slipped off her incredibly high crimson-colored heels and they hurried from the lush manicured lawn to the wooden boardwalk that took them through the protective shelter of the dunes and down to the beach.

There wasn't a soul along the sand and for that he was eternally grateful.

As they walked down the stairs at the end of the boardwalk and back around beneath it, he grabbed her shoes and placed them on the edge of the wooden boards along with his hat.

"What's up, Jase? Why did you almost drag me out of the party?" she asked and leaned against one of the thick pilings for the boardwalk.

He braced his forearm just above her head on the support and shifted until her warm breath spilled against his face. She smelled of something flowery and of Nicole and he inhaled deeply to memorize that aroma.

With his free hand, he brushed away a windblown lock of her hair and then skimmed his fingers down her smooth cheek. She trembled beneath his touch and he hardened as he imagined how smooth the rest of her skin would be and how she would shiver against him while they made love.

"I want you, Nickie."

Her eyes widened in surprise and the words rushed from her. "Hell no. I don't believe you."

"Believe it, Nickie. I've wanted you for a long time," he said and moved ever closer until his body was pressed to hers.

At that touch, she sucked in a shaky breath and closed her eyes. In a husky voice she said, "Don't play with me, Jase."

He chuckled and her eyes snapped open to meet his gaze. "Babe, I am so not playing with you. At least not yet," he said and dropped his hand to trace the rounded swells of her breasts visible above the bodice of her killer dress. It was the kind of dress that invited him to touch and to see. The fabric was fine enough that even in the dusky night, the pebbled tips of her nipples were visible.

"There's no sense in starting this. You're leaving tomorrow." She dragged in another irregular breath as he continued his caress across the sensitive skin beneath his fingers. Despite her words, as her gaze locked with his, he detected her hesitation, but also her need.

He decided to press on with his campaign to convince her that the two of them together was a good idea.

"Does everything have to be sensible with you, Nickie? Can't you just let go? Even if only for this one night? It would be good between us. I promise." To prove his point, he dipped his hand down and cupped her breast. He tweaked the tight tip between his thumb and forefinger as he pressed his body to hers and nuzzled the side of her face.

"Jase," she said on a long exhalation, but didn't move away.

His cock jumped to attention at the sound of his name on her lips. He lazily rubbed his erection across her belly and whispered into her ear, "I love the way you say my name, Nickie. Say it again. Please."

"Jase, this is crazy," she said, but she cupped his head with one hand and stroked her fingers across the short buzz of hair. She wrapped her other arm around his waist and dug her fingers into the fabric of his uniform.

"What's crazy is how long it's taken for this to happen," he said and trailed a line of kisses down her neck and across the tops of her breasts, but it wasn't enough. Not after so long.

He eased the fabric of the strapless dress down to expose her breasts and cradled them in his hands. Tenderly he teased the taut points of her nipples as he met her darkened gaze. Her hazel eyes were nearly chocolate brown with desire and she licked her lips and shot a quick glance down at his hands.

"Jase – "

"Tell me what you want, Nickie. I'll do whatever you ask . . . except stopping, that is," he teased and smiled.

* * *

Damn that boyish grin that was always my undoing, Nickie thought barely a second before she said, "Kiss me there, Jase. Please kiss me there."

With a rough groan, he dipped his head and dropped a quick kiss on the tip of each breast before alternately sucking and caressing her nipples with his mouth. Each wet tug sent a corresponding pull to between her legs where her clit pulsed and pleaded for more. She was already wet for him and every suck or bite or lick brought another wave of dampness between her thighs.

Her body shook as she held him to her and urged him on with soft cries until the sound of someone coming down the boardwalk made him pause.

He met her gaze, but instead of stopping, he inched his hand beneath the hem of her dress and continued upward, dancing his fingers along the sensitive inner skin of her thighs. When he reached her panties, he dipped his fingers inside and found the swollen bundle of nerves at her center.

"Jase," she whispered urgently and grabbed hold of his wrist as from a few feet away on the boardwalk came the murmured conversation of others.

"They can't see us. Or hear us if you're quiet. Can you be quiet, Nickie?" he asked and stroked a finger across her responsive nub, dragging a strangled moan from her.

"Or are you a screamer?" he continued and kept up his caresses, drawing her ever closer to a release.

Nickie grabbed hold of his shoulders because she needed something to keep her upright. Each shift of his fingers raised her higher and higher and weakened her knees. Her heart pounded with both excitement from his touch and fear at the thought of being discovered by whoever was still nearby on the boardwalk above them.

"Jase, please," she keened in a whisper and shot a worried look above them as the footsteps came ever closer.

He whispered against her ear, "Come for me, Nickie." He pressed against her clit and slipped a finger inside her. Stroked her urgently as he bent his head and suckled her breasts. Gently teethed the hard tips and tugged on them.

Oh God, she thought, biting her lower lip to keep from crying out as he stroked and enticed with his lips and fingers. As the juices of her release spilled over his hand and down her thighs, she wanted to scream and rip off her clothes and his and fuck him right there and then on the sand like she had in her fantasy. Even if there was someone right there watching.

From above them came another footstep and then a laugh, chilling her passion for only the short moment it took for whoever it was to head back up the boardwalk toward the house.

"They're gone, Nickie. Come for me, babe. Scream if you want," he said and shoved a second finger into her while pressing his thumb against her clit and circling it possessively.

"God, Jase. I want you inside me." She reached down and covered the long hard ridge of his erection with her hand. He groaned and laid his forehead against hers.

"Later, Nickie. I promise. Right now is all about you," he said and kissed her, his mouth warm and mobile against her lips. Coaxing her mouth open as he stroked her and slipped his tongue past her lips to taste her.

She held onto his shoulders and bucked her hips against his hand, reaching for her climax. Loving the taste and feel of his mouth against hers and his hands on her breasts and inside her. As she moved for him, the tips of her breasts rubbed against the fabric of his uniform, making them ever more sensitized and alive.

God, so alive. So damn incredible, she thought and closed her eyes, giving herself over to the sensations he was creating in her. Sensations like nothing she had ever experienced before with anyone else.

But then again, no one, anywhere, was like Jase.

"That's it, Nickie. I can feel it coming," he whispered against the shell of her ear before he bent his head to suck a spot near the crook of her shoulder.

She could feel it, too. Building inside her, higher and higher. Sending shock waves throughout her body until with one rough pull of his mouth against her skin and a sharp bite, she came.

Her body shook and trembled against his and she keened his name over and over as she shoved her hips against his hand.

"I'm here, Nickie. I'm not going anywhere," he said as he held her and gentled his caresses, letting her ease back from her release. His kisses tender and less demanding, although she knew he still wanted more.

But she wanted it, too. Her earlier hesitation about what to do with Jase was totally gone, burned away by the fire he had ignited inside her. She wanted him and if this night was to be the only night they had, she intended to make it memorable.

Chapter 4

Jason helped Nickie get presentable again, smoothing the dress back into place. Finger-brushing the long thick strands of her dark hair into some kind of order. Before they climbed back onto the boardwalk steps, he kissed her again before reluctantly breaking away.

As much as he wanted nothing more than to make love to her all night long, there were still guests up at the house and responsibilities to be handled. Nickie was not the kind of woman that would fail to honor those duties.

He snagged his hat and her shoes from the boardwalk and they walked hand-in-hand back to the mansion. Many of the guests had left and there was only one couple outside on the terrace as they approached. He was grateful for that. He wanted to be alone with her for as long as possible.

As they reached the edge of the lawn and the steps to the flagstone, he urged Nickie back into his arms and kissed her again, reminding her that this was only a short break from the night they would spend together.

"I'll meet you in your room later," he said when they separated.

"When, Jase? People are going to linger – "

He laid a finger against those lush lips he wanted to kiss all night long. "You head up and I'll be there, Nickie. I promise."

She nodded, her doubt obvious, but he kissed her once more to reassure her. When they parted, she went inside to mingle with the guests while he took a calming breath to curb the erection that refused to go away as long as she was near.

It took several long minutes and lots of thoughts about baseball scores until he could venture back inside. Somehow he managed to plaster on a smile and make nice with the remaining guests until little by little the number of people dwindled down to just them and a few long distance family members waiting to say their goodbyes before they headed to a nearby hotel. He and his parents had been invited to stay with the de Silvas because they were in some ways closer than distant family.

"Thank you for your hospitality, Mr. and Mrs. de Silva," he said to Nickie's parents as he and his parents stood by the stairway just past midnight. Nickie and Tommy waited there as well, completing their familial duties, although a bright flush of color erupted along Nickie's cheeks as she shot him a quick look.

"It's our pleasure, Jason. You're family," Mrs. de Silva replied.

Nickie's dad grudgingly agreed, but shot him a hairy eyeball before likewise glancing at his daughter. He clearly sensed there was more going on than was obvious and judging from his glare, he wasn't too thrilled about it.

"I guess we'll see you in the morning," his mother said and after all the parents hugged, he dutifully followed his up the stairs, but he had every intention of changing and sneaking back out to Nickie's room as he had promised.

At the door to his parents' room, he embraced them and offered a good night before entering the bedroom next to them. Their accommodations were located in the west wing of the beachside mansion while the de Silva family quarters were on the opposite end of the building. The grand staircase split the floors in half and there was no way he'd make it down the hall to Nickie's room at the far end of the wing without being seen.

That was the last thing either of them wanted right now. Whatever was happening was still too fragile for such scrutiny.

Inside his room, he quickly stripped and hung up his dress uniform and sword. A sense of pride filled him for a moment to see them and all that they represented. He'd met the challenge and succeeded.

Now it was time to face another challenge in his life.

He quickly changed into black jeans, a black polo shirt, and sneakers for traction. His room opened onto a balcony that faced the ocean and ran the length of their wing. The de Silva family section had a similar balcony, but the two weren't connected.

That wasn't about to stop him. He'd scaled higher and harder places during some of his ROTC training assignments.

He shut off his lights and exited onto the balcony, careful to keep out of sight. A trellis at the far side of the space was covered with fragrant wisteria. The thick tangle of the plant's vines provided an easy way to climb down to the ground floor and the fragrant blooms would provide some cover to keep him from being seen. Luckily the bees wouldn't be buzzing around the flowers at night.

On the flagstone terrace he skirted the edges and watched as Nickie and her family bid the last of their guests good night. Together they trudged up the stairs and into their wing of the home.

He waited until the lights snapped on in the various rooms and easily identified Nickie's as he caught sight of her silhouette by the French doors leading onto the balcony. He jogged toward the wisteria-covered trellis close to her room and scrambled up the tangle of vines and over the railing.

At her French doors, he rapped lightly on a glass pane and barely a heartbeat later, she cracked open the door and let him enter.

* * *

Nickie had told herself all night long that Jase wouldn't keep his promise. That he'd rethink what he'd done earlier and decide that she just wasn't the kind of woman for a man like him. A man who took risks. A man of action and not hesitation.

But having him standing there, looking dangerously sexy in all black, told her otherwise.

"I didn't think you'd actually come," she said and defensively wrapped her arms around her waist.

"I made a promise, Nickie. I keep my promises," he said and stepped close.

But all he'd promised was tonight and I'm not a one night stand kind of girl, she thought. Almost as if he could read her mind, he said, "Don't run from this before we even get started."

She chuckled hesitantly and offered up a hesitant smile. "Seems to me we already got started beneath the boardwalk."

He grinned and laid a hand by the crook of her neck. He urged her forward until they were barely inches apart. He smelled like sunshine and the beach and she breathed that scent in deeply. The weight of his hand on her neck was demanding, but in a good way, and sent a thrill through her. Between her legs, her clit throbbed for his touch and she grew damp again.

"I guess we did, babe. So are you ready for more?"

"That depends."

He narrowed his amazing green eyes and examined her features. "That depends on what?"

She was nothing if not honest. "On what *you* want to do."

He grinned again and she realized that sex with him would always be filled with light and laughter and fun. "Let's start off easy, Nickie. I want you to talk dirty to me."

"Talk dirty?"

He expects me, a woman who blushes at the good spots in romance novels, to talk dirty?

"Like this," he said and finally closed the last few inches between them and his warm breath tickled her skin as he whispered in her ear. "I love your tits. The way they feel in my hands and in my mouth. I'm so hard thinking about how they'll taste again and how they'll move as you ride me later."

She moaned and beneath her dress, her nipples pebbled almost painfully, aching for his touch and his wonderful mouth.

"You so don't play fair, Jase."

"I'm always fair, Nickie. You know that, but I'm also determined to get what I want and I want you. So will you do it?" he asked and bit her earlobe playfully. "Will you talk dirty to me?"

"Christ, Jase. You know this is difficult for me," she said and he surprised her by grabbing hold of her hand and pressing it over the long ridge of his erection.

"You don't know how difficult it was to see you all night long and ignore the fact that what I wanted the most was to be buried inside you."

She moaned at that thought and cupped his cock, getting even wetter as she imagined him filling her. Somehow she found the courage to say the words he wanted to hear.

"I used to watch you on the beach with Tommy and wonder what you'd look like. How you'd feel in my hand, like you do now," she said and stroked him. Explored the length and width of him as best as she could with the fabric of the jeans keeping her from his erection.

"That's it, babe. Oh God, that's it," he said, urging her on as he stood stock still in front of her, as if understanding that if he did another thing, she might reconsider their night together.

"You're so big, Jase. All of you," she said and she ran her free hand across the broad width of his shoulders and then down to cup the thick muscles on his chest. He was well over six foot and without her killer heels, the top of her head barely brushed his chin. She raised her head and brushed a kiss along the rasp of beard on his jaw.

"I want to see you, Jase. Feel your skin," she said.

She'd fantasized about it so often in her dreams and as she'd sat on the beach reading, although a good part of her attention had been on him as he'd worked the lifeguard stand or surfed. He was so beautiful and she'd wondered more than once how his board shorts had stayed on those lean hips. She had sweated more than once as the shorts had dipped low to reveal those enticing Vees that temptingly pointed down.

At her words, he went into action, ripping off his sweater to reveal his chest, immense shoulders, and a defined six pack that was more of an eight pack and would put any cover model to shame.

She laid her hands on his shoulders before moving them all across those muscles and his smooth hot skin. Beneath her hands he was tense and as she met his gaze, she realized just how much he wanted her and how much control he was exerting.

She also realized for the first time just how much control she had over him.

It was more exciting than she could ever have imagined.

Emboldened, she said, "I'm wet for you, Jase. Wet and aching for you to touch me again."

"Only if you want me to, Nickie. I'll never do anything you don't want me to do," he said, his hands fisted at his sides as he struggled for restraint.

She shuddered with need and dipped her hands down to the waistband of his black jeans, but she couldn't go any further. Not just yet. Holding onto the waistband as if it was a life preserver, she met his gaze and said, "I don't know what I want. I don't normally play these kinds of games."

* * *

Serious bookish Nickie would never play a game quite like this one, Jase thought.

Not that he did either. He wasn't the kind of guy who had fuck buddies or used women for hook-ups.

"This isn't a game, Nickie. This is for real. What I feel for you is for real, but I want you to enjoy it. And I need for you to want me as much as I want you."

"I do, Jase. I just need a little . . . guidance," she said, more shyly than he could have anticipated.

"Guidance, huh? I guess if there's one thing I've learned in the military, it's how to give orders," he said mischievously.

He was relieved when she grinned and playfully saluted him.

"Yes, I guess you have, Lieutenant."

Smiling, he said, "Take off your dress, babe. I've waited way too long to see you."

With surprising speed considering her earlier shyness, she unzipped the dress and let it drop to the hard wood floor in a pool of crimson. She stood before him, her upper body naked and a small lacy black panty covering her hips. Those long legs he'd fantasized about were likewise bare.

"Come here," he commanded and pointed to a spot on the floor just before him.

She did as he asked and stood there, expectant. The tips of her breasts were hard and just waiting for him. His mouth watered at the thought of them, but he held back, suddenly needing more from her and knowing she wanted more from him.

"Touch yourself, Nickie. Touch your tits," he commanded and she hesitated, but then reached up and cupped her breasts. Ran her fingers across the tips and tweaked them into even harder points. His cock swelled inside his jeans and the pressure of the fabric against his erection was almost painful.

"God, that's it, Nickie. You're so fucking beautiful," he said with a groan and undid his zipper to free his cock from the jeans and his briefs. He stroked his hand up and down its length, imaging how her hands would feel on him. How he'd feel buried inside her.

She watched him, her gaze darkening as she did so, and as she continued to touch herself which only made him harder. Made him stroke faster as he said, "Your tits are so sweet, Nickie. I can't wait to taste them again."

She surprised him by suddenly saying, "I want to see you, Jase. All of you."

He didn't hesitate. He shucked off his jeans and briefs and positioned himself next to her, skin to skin. The tips of her breasts brushing against his chest and his dick tucked against the softness of her belly and the lace of the panties. He eased his hand beneath the fabric and found her center. Danced his fingers across her lips and clit, dragging her eyes shut as she shook against him.

"Open your eyes, Nickie. I want you to watch me touch you."

Her eyelids flitted up and down before she did as he asked and fixed her gaze on his hand as he moved it against her. He pressed his fingers against her swollen nub and wet lips. After, he eased one finger and then another into her tightness and she moaned, grabbed hold of his wrist to stop him.

"Jase, please. I can't – "

"You can, Nickie. You can come for me again and again and again," he said. He grabbed hold of her waist with his free hand and inched her back toward the bed as her knees weakened from his continued caresses.

When her hips were on the bed, he ripped off her panties and urged her legs open, exposing her to him. Her lips were flushed a rosy pink and moist; her mound swollen and aching to be touched. She wasn't waxed or trimmed to death and as he stroked his fingers across her, he liked the softness of her midnight curls beneath his hand.

She lifted her hips and whimpered in anticipation.

"Ah, Nickie, I'm so hard for you," he said and stroked himself while he continued to fondle her.

Her gaze dipped to his cock and she watched silently for a moment, but then raised herself up on one arm and covered the head of his dick with her hand. Pre-cum escaped him and she spread that wet all across his head and dragged a finger across the underside of his penis and the sensitive spot there.

That simple touch rocked his world. He blew out a harsh breath, gritted his teeth, and said, "God, Nickie. Not yet, babe. Not yet."

He ripped away from her and bent to brush a trail of kisses up her inner thighs and to the nest of dark curls. He kissed the bundle of nerves at her center and encircled her thighs with his arms, holding her tight to his mouth. Sucking, nibbling, and licking.

Easing a finger into her as he had earlier that night and finding her tight, but slick and ready for more.

* * *

Nickie raised her hips against his mouth, lost in the pleasure he was bringing her, but wanting his thick long cock inside her as she came. Wanting the warmth and wet of his mouth on her breasts.

"Touch your tits, Nickie," he ordered again and his gaze locked on her as she cupped her breasts and played with them. Each little tweak reverberated through her and inside her pussy which clenched in anticipation.

"I can feel it. I can feel how much you want me," he said, pressing his fingers deeper and opening her for another kind of possession.

She mewled and shoved against him with her hips while she continued to play with herself, waiting for him. Ready to take his beautiful cock deep inside.

"I'm safe, Nickie. Are you protected?" he asked as he rose and his cock brushed across her center.

She whimpered in anticipation and nodded. Watched as he guided his erection to her center. The tip of him kissed her clit and lips before he eased just his head inside her pussy.

She moaned at the feel of him, so warm and making her feel so full with just that first tentative entry.

He shuddered and closed his eyes as she surrounded the head of his cock with her pussy. Bracing his hands on her thighs, he struggled for control and sucked in a rough breath before opening his eyes. His irises had gone to such a deep emerald, it was almost impossible to see where they ended and his pupils began.

"I've waited so long for this," he said and then he eased the rest of his length inside in one smooth lazy push.

She came immediately from the pressure and friction of his penetration.

Her body shook and she cried out as waves of pleasure swept over her. She clamped her thighs against his hips to hold him still, savoring her release, but guilt instantly slammed into her that she hadn't waited for him.

"I'm sorry, Jase. So sorry."

She met his gaze, so dark now from his own desire. He smiled and raised a shaky hand to cradle her cheek. Her musky aroma clung to his long agile fingers.

"That was amazing, Nickie. And we're not done yet. Not by a long shot," he said and shifted his hips, pulling out of her before slowly driving back in.

She hadn't thought it possible for desire to rise up again so quickly, but it did. Each sure stroke of his hips sent a shock wave through her body until she was arching up against him, accepting each powerful thrust. Nearly crying out as he found her clit with his thumb and the pressure of his finger there caressed her with each rock of his hips.

"Let it out, Nickie. Scream for me, babe. Scream my name."

She held onto his shoulders and wrapped her legs around his hips which heightened the press of his thumb against her and the penetration of his cock. She met his gaze for only a second before another release slammed into her and she gave him what he wanted.

"Ja-a-a-s-s-s-e," she cried out and dug her fingers into his shoulders to hold on as the world around her shattered. Through the haze of her pleasure, she heard, "God, Nickie. You feel so fuckin' amazing. You're so beautiful when you come."

With a rough groan of his own and a few wild jerks of his hips, he shouted out her name as he came. "Nickie."

His big body tensed and stilled as his warmth spilled inside her. His cock throbbed and twitched against her pussy as the lingering aftershocks of her release caressed him.

She smoothed her hands across his sweat-damp shoulders and his strong muscles trembled beneath her palms. She urged him down until he was resting against her and they were both half-on and half-off her bed, but too shaken to move. Unwilling to break apart so they could relish the remnants of their pleasure.

He kissed her tenderly and started to say something, but then stopped. In a way, she understood. She didn't have the right words for what had just happened. For how she was feeling. She didn't want to diminish the experience with anything less than the perfect words.

With a smile, she shifted her hands across the short strands of his hair and returned the kiss. Happy to let that simple act convey all that she was feeling.

They lingered there, still joined, until nature took matters into its own hands and he slipped from her.

Wordlessly, they moved beneath the blankets and to the center of her bed.

She lay there, facing him, both hesitant and expectant until he laid a hand at her waist and soothed it up and down her side in a reassuring caress.

"Are you worried that I'll leave or that I'll stay?"

Chapter 5

A myriad of emotions flashed across Nickie's expressive face.

She'd never been good at hiding her feelings and that hadn't changed, Jase thought.

With the barest shrug of a fine-boned shoulder, she said, "A little bit of each."

He totally understood. Every second spent with her like this was a second to be treasured, but also a second that made the thought of leaving her tomorrow even harder. "I get what you're feeling. This isn't easy for me either."

"So why do this, Jase? This is an impossible situation," she said and the glint of tears filmed over the dark hazel of her gaze.

He cupped her cheek and smoothed his thumb across it, trying to offer comfort. "I don't believe in impossible, babe. I never have. This won't be easy, I'll give you that, but I think it's worth it. Don't you?"

A ghost of a smile flitted across her lips before it blossomed into a big smile that chased away her tears. "Yeah, I do, Jase. I think it's worth it."

He grinned and hauled her close, and she pillowed her head on his one arm and twined her legs with his. She wrapped one arm around his waist and tucked the other beneath his head as they lay there, facing each other. Still feeling the uncertainty of new lovers and the eternal "WTF do we do now?" in the aftermath of their lovemaking.

Jase's stomach settled it for them with a loud growl.

He spread his hand across his midsection, chuckled, and grinned. "The party pickin's were good, but not very filling."

"I'm a little hungry, too. How about I go get some food?" she said, but she was in motion before he could answer, grabbing her robe and rushing to her door.

Like he had before, he understood where she was mentally. She needed a little bit of time to gather herself. To understand why she was doing something so totally out of character and as she had said, something seemingly impossible.

So he lay back against her pillows and waited, hoping that the time alone wouldn't give her an opportunity to reconsider her earlier emotions.

* * *

Nickie closed the door to her bedroom and leaned against the wall, sucking in a deep breath to calm the maelstrom of feelings swirling around in her head and heart.

Nothing could have ever prepared her for what it was like to be with Jase. Nothing. It was better than anything she could have imagined with the power to bring joy, but also to destroy her. She knew that now. She wasn't just giving him her body, she was giving him her heart and soul and that brought the possibility of lots of pain if things didn't work out.

They'd already admitted that what came next wasn't going to be easy.

She still had years to complete in medical school and he had years to serve to pay back the costs for his college tuition.

Years of separation, she thought, her throat tight with emotion.

She finally pushed off the wall and headed toward the kitchen, telling herself not to logic herself out of one of the most amazing and rewarding things that had ever happened to her.

In the kitchen she grabbed a breakfast tray and loaded it up with an assortment of the foods that had been left over from the party. Cheeses and fruits. A small plate with some finger sandwiches. There was an almost full bottle of red wine on the counter and she snagged it and two glasses.

The tray was heavy as she trudged back upstairs with it and somehow managed a one-handed hold to open the door to her room.

For a moment she panicked as she stepped in and saw that her bed was empty, but then she realized that Jase was lounging on the small loveseat by the French doors leading to the balcony. He had put his jeans back on, but they were unbuttoned and showing off an enticing amount of skin and a little happy trail of blonde hair down the middle of his lower abdomen. He was bare-chested and his arms were crossed behind his head which made all those sculpted muscles even more defined.

Her heart thumped wildly at the sight of him. He was just so beautiful.

And he was hers. No more doubts or hesitation or worries.

He was hers for at least tonight and she didn't intend to spend another moment of their time together doubting the wonder of that. She'd deal with the heartache later.

She hurried over and placed the tray on the small coffee table in front of the loveseat. Teasingly she said, "Make yourself at home."

He grinned and patted the space beside him. "The bed was too lonely without you."

She guffawed and rolled her eyes. "Does that line ever really work with anyone?"

His grin broadened, deepening the dimple on one side and making him look boyish again. "Very few anyones to try it on, Nickie."

She tried not to let his comment please her so much and to keep the lighthearted mood going, she elbowed him playfully. "I'm sure the girls at 'Nova were literally falling at your feet so give it a rest, Hart."

He dropped his arms to draped them over the back and arm of the loveseat and said, "Okay, here I am, resting. Literally. Feed me, Nickie. Please. I'm too weak to go on without some food."

She chuckled and shook her head. She grabbed a small bunch of the grapes and held them to his lips like Eve tempting Adam. He tugged one off with his perfect white teeth and she pulled another one from the bunch and popped it into her mouth.

"Sweet," she said as the juices exploded in her mouth.

Jase grinned and after she swallowed, surged forward and kissed her. Dipped his tongue in and murmured, "You're way sweeter." He lingered then, coaxing her lips to open with his. Sucking and biting at her lower lip until she was leaning into him, wanting more.

She moaned a protest as he shifted away, but he merely shot her that devil-may-care smile again and grabbed a few pieces of cheese. "While you're way more tempting, I really do need some food."

Tempting, huh?

Feeling decidedly more dangerous than she ever had, she leaned over to snare a piece of cheese, giving him an eyeful of what was beneath her robe. Or should she say what wasn't beneath her robe. Even with her downcast gaze, she didn't fail to miss how he admired her nakedness and how the green of his eyes darkened once more with desire.

Empowered, she eased back to her seat, but trailed her hand down his thigh, appreciating the strength of the rock hard muscle beneath the faded black denim.

"That's a dangerous move, Nickie," he warned, the tones of his voice husky which stirred something alive in her.

"Is it, Jase?" she teased and stroked her hand up his thigh again, letting her thumb skim along the edge of his steadily growing erection.

* * *

Jase didn't fail to miss the new boldness in her and as she grazed his cock with her finger, it hardened instantly with that barest touch. Despite that, he held back, determined to take it slow with her. She might be all full of fire now, but he knew her too well not to recognize that she might regret some things come the morning.

Regret was the last thing he wanted her to take away from tonight.

Reaching over, he poured glasses of wine and handed one to her, wanting her to have something to do with her hands that didn't involve his dick. At least for right now. He needed a moment to recover in more ways than one.

She made a moue with her mouth, obviously displeased and clearly aware of his ploy. "I don't get it, Jase. I thought you wanted this night – "

"I do, but I don't want to rush things. We still have lots of night and morning left, babe."

Her hazel gaze warmed, but mischief glittered in her eyes. She nodded and sipped her wine. Reached over and grabbed a finger sandwich that she offered to him. Some of the ham spread from the sandwich smeared on her finger and she licked it off.

His mind pictured her licking him with that beautiful wet tongue and his dick jerked in his jeans.

He swallowed and took a big gulp of his wine. Leaning over, he picked up another small sandwich that he fed to her. As she ate it from his hand, he said, "Your parents sure know how to throw a bash."

She wrinkled her nose and glanced away. "Seems like there might be better things to do with all that money."

"Like?" he asked, although he was well aware of where she was going. Nickie had always been almost ashamed of what she had, not that her family was obnoxious about their money. The mansion, while on the beach and large, was like many others along this wealthy strip of the Jersey Shore. Tommy and she had gone to the local high school, not some fancy private school and unlike some of the other rich kids they rarely showed off with outrageously priced designer duds or over-the-top jewelry. Maybe it was because their dad had worked hard for his money and wasn't keen on wasting it on unnecessary luxuries.

She lifted one shoulder and nonchalantly said, "Like stuff. Lord knows we have enough of that."

"You're not that bad, Nickie."

"I guess. I just feel . . ."

"Guilty? Why? Because you have and people like me don't?" he said and anger welled up within him. He'd never let the differences between them be an issue, but she was making it impossible to ignore those differences now. "I don't need a pity party, Nickie. If that's why you're here with me, just to be a fuck buddy to poor little me – "

"That's not why I'm here, damn it. I'm here because I care for you. I just can't stand the thought that for the next four years you're going to have to risk your life just because you wanted to get a college degree." Her voice was tight, her frustration apparent and once again, the hint of unshed tears shimmered in her gaze.

He wrapped his arm around her neck and hauled her tight to his chest. Embracing her, he kissed her forehead and said, "I'm a Marine because I want to be. I could have gotten some other kind of scholarship, but I wanted to do this. *I needed* to do this. I know that's hard to understand for some – "

"No, it isn't. I guess I get it, but I'm not sure I like it, Jase," she admitted.

"We're more alike than you think, Nickie. You wanted to make a difference so you decided to go to medical school. I needed to make a difference also and this is how I can do it."

She glanced at him, a watery smile on her face. "Yeah, I know you can, Jase. I know you'll keep your men safe, but I want you to keep yourself safe as well."

He bent his head and kissed her, his touch tender and full of promise. She tasted of the wine and of Nickie. It was a taste he'd keep with him during all those times they'd be apart.

Slowly the kiss deepened, until they were both straining toward one another, needing to take it to the next level.

Easing her away, he said, "This loveseat really wasn't made for what I had in mind."

His roguish words had the desired effect. She grinned and rose. Held out her hand and he laced his fingers with hers and walked back to the bed with her.

Gracefully she eased off her robe and let it drop to the floor, exposing the long elegant line of her back. She climbed into the center of the bed where she waited for him. Her skin was a creamy color against the stark white of the sheets, her hair a dark spill across the disarray of the pillows. The tips of her breasts were tight again and a darker rose color against the delightful flush spreading across her body.

God, but she was so beautiful and for tonight, and hopefully longer, she was his.

He shucked off his jeans, kicked them away, and hurried to her side. In seconds they were a tangle of arms and legs and urgent kisses. It took all of his restraint not to drive himself deep inside her, but he wanted her with him when he came. And he didn't want to rush since this might possibly be the only night they'd have together for some time.

Urging her onto her side, he spooned against her back while he reached around her body. He played her with his hands, caressing and tweaking her breasts while he fondled her clit. He dragged his fingers back and forth across the dampness and the responsive bud at her core.

She was wet down there, so so wet that he almost came just from the thought of all that warm moist surrounding him. Especially as the rising rush of her release registered against his hand. Her pussy vibrated and clenched around his fingers, slick and inviting.

He groaned and fought back his own desire as his cock jumped and swelled against the small of her back.

"Easy, Nickie, easy, babe," he said softly and gave one last stroke with his hand along her hot moist center.

She moaned and pushed back against him, inviting him to join with her again. "Please, Jase. I want you inside me."

Easing one thigh between hers, he guided himself to her pussy and slowly pressed in, gritting his teeth at the sheer pleasure of being joined with her. She was hot. Sleek. Her pussy accepted him as he buried himself to the hilt and held still, enjoying the way she caressed him.

His body was flush against the velvety skin of her back. Their legs tangled together as he ground into her, deepening his possession.

Her urgent cry was hard to resist, as was the way she gripped his thigh, but he held back from pulling out and driving back into her.

Leaning over her, he dropped a kiss against the side of face and whispered, "Tell me what you feel, Nickie."

* * *

Words, emotions, and sensations pummeled Nickie's mind, making speech impossible.

"Tell me, Nickie," he pressed again, in command again as he had been earlier.

"Full, so full," she said and tried to move her hips, but he splayed his hand against her belly and stopped her.

"What else, babe?" he said, but as steady as he was trying to be, his body trembled beside hers and inside, his cock jerked and swelled even more, stretching her to the point of pleasure-pain.

"You know what else, Jase," she said and moaned as he finally moved inside her, shifting out and then back in slowly. The friction of that motion creating heat throughout her pussy, which throbbed and tightened around him.

"Do you want me to tell you what I feel, Nickie? Is that what you want?" he asked and circled his hips, heightening his possession. Drawing a rough shudder from her as her climax threatened to take them both over.

God, yes, she wanted him to tell her because she couldn't say the words. Couldn't free herself to be that kind of woman.

"Don't, Nickie. Don't pull back," he urged.

She held onto his words, braved past her fears, and murmured, "Tell me, Jase. Tell me what you feel."

He sucked in a breath and the words exploded from his mouth. "I love how hot you are. How wet. The way your pussy holds me tight. My balls are hard for you, Nickie. So so hard. Feel them. Touch them."

She reached down between their bodies and cupped him. His balls were tight and she massaged them, earning a long groan from him.

"That's it, Nickie. God, that's it, babe," he said before he bent and kissed her. Nipped and licked at her lips as he finally moved, driving in and out of her. Repeating the motion at her sharp gasp of pleasure.

"Jase, that feels so good," she keened and he increased his pace, pistoning his hips as he drove them ever higher until with one deep thrust, they came together, bodies shaking. Sweat bathing them as he wrapped his arms around her and kept her tight to him.

"God, Nickie. Don't move. I want to be with you forever," he said and his body shuddered around her.

She laid her arms over his and snuggled back into him, the fullness of him within her satisfying even as the lingering vibrations from her climax faded away. But little by little he softened and finally, regretfully, he left her and she turned and faced him.

He grinned, her beautiful man. She ran her hand across the sandpapery roughness of his cheek and along the short crisp hairs along the sides of his head. "You are so . . . amazing, Jase. So special . . ."

And you deserve a woman who can be as amazing and special as you are, she thought and looked down to avoid his perceptive gaze. But he wasn't going to let her escape that easily.

Jase cradled her jaw and applied gentle pressure to urge her head back up. "What's wrong, Nickie? Why are you so upset? This was like nothing I've ever felt before with anyone."

"But this isn't the real me. I can't be the kind of woman you want. That you need. I'm not brave. I'm not bold. I'm just . . . me," she said, tears thick in her voice. Her throat was so tight with emotion, it was almost suffocating her.

The ghost of a smile played about his lips and he tunneled his fingers through her hair. "'Me' is all I want, Nickie. You don't need to be anything but yourself with me."

"Why do I find that hard to believe, Jase? If this night has been about anything – "

"It's been about admitting who you are, nothing more. It's about not having any regrets, because I know I would have regretted never getting to spend this time with you," he said, cradled her sides and drew her even closer.

She buried her face against his chest, unable to face him, but more importantly, not sure how to face herself. She didn't want regrets either, but everything seemed to be moving too quickly. More quickly than she could handle at the moment.

He wrapped his arms around her and held her gently, his touch calming and filled with tenderness. He brushed a kiss across the top of her head and whispered, "I won't push anymore, Nickie, because I don't want to push you away with my demands."

He had been demanding and in command, but only because she had allowed him to take the lead. It brought back a quote she'd once heard about no one being able to make you feel inferior unless you let them. She'd let him be in charge, but at the same time, she'd never felt like less than an equal in everything that had been going on. And she'd known that at any time she could stop and he wouldn't press.

Much like he wasn't pressing now, but only offering comfort and support.

He relaxed beside her, the tension exiting his big body and minutes later, a soft snore escaped him. She smiled at that because it somehow humanized him even more, this gorgeous perfect man she had wanted for so long. Who she had loved for way too long.

So what am I going to do about it? About him? she wondered as she lay there, surrounded by the peace of his embrace. Tomorrow he'd be going home with his parents and after, heading to Afghanistan. It would be months before he was home again.

She wouldn't think about the possibility of his not coming home alive.

Jase wasn't only a doer, he was a thinker. A leader. He never acted without a plan or took unnecessary risks.

But it occurred to her that he had taken a risk on her tonight. He had put his heart on the line, only she hadn't been able to reciprocate fully. She hadn't been able to risk her heart the way he had.

Which left her with the kind of choice she normally avoided: take a chance or walk away filled with doubt and wondering "What if. . .?"

As she peered toward her nightstand, her alarm clock warned her that she had to make a decision soon. The night was rushing away from them, far faster than she ever could have imagined.

It was time for her to take a chance. . .

Chapter 6

Something tickled the side of his face and Jase scrunched his neck up to chase it away. Her sexy giggle teased him awake.

"Come on, sleepyhead. We don't have much time left," Nickie said with tempting huskiness.

It took him a moment to make sense of where he was and what was happening, beginning with her giggle and sexiness, both distinctively out-of-character.

He barely lifted one lid and risked a glance at the alarm clock. 4 a.m.

Not even the Marines made him get up that early.

"Come on, Jase," she urged again. Her warm hands palmed his pectorals and she whispered a kiss across his cheek. Nuzzled the side of his face with her nose and giggled again before the mattress shifted with her movement.

He opened his eyes and found her sitting on the edge of the bed. She had on a flowery beach cover-up and her bathing suit, and a large blanket sat in her lap. Even with all the clothes covering her body, lots and lots of skin was visible and with it being morning and all, his body reacted, tenting the sheets covering him. Drawing her gaze to his dick, so he rolled onto his side, knowing from their last lovemaking that she was a little uneasy with all that was happening between them.

"It's a little early for the beach, isn't it?" he asked, propped his head on one hand and finger-combed the longer top strands into place with the other.

"It's not too early for what I had in mind," she said and stroked a hand across his chest and down, taking the sheet with her as she moved south and wrapped a hand around his cock.

He gently grasped her wrist and stopped her. "What are you doing, Nickie?"

"No regrets, you said. So I'm doing what I've wanted to for a very long time."

He arched a brow and examined her now serious features. "Which is?"

"Seducing you. Well at least that's what I'd do if you'd get your too cute ass out of bed and come with me," she said with a roll of her eyes and a sharp, almost annoyed breath.

This was finally his Nickie, the one full of humor and spirit.

"Well, since you asked so nicely," he said, sat up and ripped away the sheet, exposing his fully alert cock to her attention.

Her gaze drifted downward and she licked her lips, but a second later, she tossed his briefs into his lap. "You'll have to hide that thing for just a little longer."

"Whatever you say, Nickie. You're in command now," he said, saluted her and a delighted smile erupted across her lips. The gold flecks in her hazel eyes glittered brightly.

"Yes, yes I am, Jase. I'm in control now and I kind of like it."

He grinned and hauled her close for a brief hard kiss. "I do, too," he said.

* * *

With the way he was looking at her and the sight of him aroused, Nickie almost reconsidered acting out her fantasy, but she'd made herself a promise in the dark of night as she lay there beside him.

When morning came, she'd finally take matters, and Jase, into her own hands without any doubt or hesitation keeping her from showing him just how much she wanted him. Just how much she cared for him.

Grabbing hold of his hand, she led him to the door of her room, but he hesitated at the entrance. "What if someone sees us?"

"It's 4 a.m. and what if they do?" she teased, finally feeling free now that she'd made her decision about him.

"Does your father still have that shotgun?" he kidded even as they snuck down the hall and quietly crept toward the stairs.

"Yes, he does, but I'm still not risking my life on that wisteria trellis," she tossed back over her shoulder, continuing to drag him along, down the stairs, and through the great room.

They hurried out the back door and past the terrace and lawn. Almost ran the length of the boardwalk and through the dunes until they were on the moonlit beach. A thankfully empty beach at that early hour.

Together they spread out the blanket she had brought by a large marsh grass-covered dune. The dune was high enough to hide their presence from anyone up at the house and possibly even from any people idly walking down the beach since they were tucked behind part of it.

She didn't waste a moment to pull him near and playfully tug off his briefs, although they snagged on his deliciously erect cock for a moment. Once he was naked, she shrugged off her cover-up, placed her hands on his shoulders, and urged him down to the blanket where she kneeled beside him.

He tucked his hands beneath his head, making his broad chest look even bigger and more powerful. The muscles in his arms were bunched from the action and she tentatively ran her hands across his arms, exploring the hard biceps. Shifting to his shoulders, and then to his sculpted chest muscles.

She cupped him and stroked her thumbs across the tight nub of his masculine nipples, earning a soft sigh from him.

"I like that, Nickie," he said and his gaze dipped down to watch her.

She licked her lips, knowing what she had fantasized about doing next, but wanting to please him. "What else do you like, Jase?"

He looked up at her and his gaze drifted over her lips, as powerful as one of his kisses. Her stomach did a flip flop and heat flared through her.

"You kissing me. I like that a lot," he said.

She bent and opened her mouth against his while she continued caressing his nipples. Tweaking and rubbing those hard nubs and loving his masculine grunt of pleasure.

His mouth was mobile beneath hers and she slipped her tongue past the seam of his lips and danced her tongue with his. Eased away and tempted him with a quick nip of his lower lip before accepting the slide of his tongue into her.

As she imagined him sliding his cock into her, she moaned and broke away for a shaky breath. She leaned over him until the tips of her breasts rubbed across his chest and her nipples tightened beneath the fabric of her bathing suit.

"Put your hands on me, Nickie," he whispered against her lips and she trailed her hand down his center to encircle his dick. She stroked him, alternately long sweeps up and down his length with a teasing circle around his sensitive head until they were both breathing heavily and his cock was even bigger and harder in her hand.

"What else, Jase? Tell me what else you want," she said, taking control as he had done earlier.

"You've got too many clothes on, babe," he said and finally moved his hands to behind her neck where with a quick pull, he undid the strings at her neck and back. Her top dropped off and onto his abs, a bright confection of pink, orange, and green against his tanned skin.

He skimmed it off his midsection on the way to her breasts. He cupped them and strummed his fingers against her nipples. Pulled them into hard little points that he tweaked, sending sharp little tugs of need straight to her center. But she wasn't going to rush this.

She wanted to live her fantasy, if only for this one night. She'd deal with the heartbreak later.

She undid the strings on her bottom and let it slide off as she straddled his thighs and sat up, staring down at him. Her hand on his cock, she stroked him while he caressed her breasts.

"You know what I want, Jase?" she asked and glanced at his erection. He had a beautiful cock, long and smooth. Thick enough to fit perfectly between her hands as she ran them up and down his shaft, giving him pleasure.

"Why don't you show me what you want," he said and lifted his hips, pushing against her hands.

She didn't refuse, bending and shimmying back along his legs so she could lick all around the sensitive head of his cock and to his F spot underneath. He groaned and jerked his hips upward, but she took her time with him, exploring every inch. Licking and sucking at him while she continued to caress his shaft with one hand and dropped the other to his tight perfect balls.

His guttural cries spurred her on as did the touch of his hands on her breasts, kneading and teasing the tips.

She took him in deeper, filling her mouth with him and he pushed up with his hips and cradled her head in his hands, his back arching. The first taste of him coming against her tongue was salty. She shifted and licked it away from the head of his cock before opening her throat and taking him in even deeper.

His body shook beneath her and he let out a long, rough growl of pleasure.

"Fuck, Nickie. I can't hold on, babe. I need you," he said, slipped his hands beneath her arms and urged her up.

"Ride me, Nickie. Make me come," he said, a low needy rumble threaded through his words, much like her fantasy Jase, but this was no dream.

He was here and he was hers.

She straddled him and reached down to guide him to her center. The dampness there wet his dick as she positioned him at her core and then drove down urgently, needing him inside as much as he wanted to be there.

With a rough inhalation, she savored the fullness of him and ground down onto him, rocking from side to side as if to work him even deeper.

He gripped her hips hard. So hard she knew there would be bruises there later, but she'd welcome those marks. Use them to remember this night until they faded from sight, but the memories of this time together would never fade.

She rocked her hips, taking him in and out, her pace slow and steady at first, but growing ever wilder and more frantic as they both reached for their release. He met each of her thrusts with his own, rising up to deepen his penetration. Guiding her with those hard hands, his gaze locked on her face. All traces of boyishness gone from his features as he strove for his pleasure and hers.

The night was soon filled with the sounds of their lovemaking. Their rough sighs and murmured cries of desire. The slap of her body against his as she rode him and his gaze dipped from her face to her breasts.

She remembered his words about how he wanted to watch her tits move as she rode him and her pussy clenched around him with that thought.

"Christ, that feels amazing, Nickie. You look amazing, riding me," he said, the tones of his voice low and husky.

He rose up then and sucked her nipples. He teased the tips with his mouth and teeth until it was no longer possible to hold back her release.

It came like fireworks on a Fourth of July night, bright, loud, and surprising. Exploding across them with an intense burst of pleasure followed by tinier flares all across their bodies. By the time the last little embers died away, they were both still breathing heavily, as if they'd run for miles.

Nickie stretched out across him, careful not to break the union with him. Wanting to stay joined as long as she could as she nestled against his chest. He was damp with sweat and so was she, but she knew just how to remedy that situation. But not until a little later.

She wanted to savor this moment for as long as she could.

He wrapped his arms around her waist and said, "I don't ever want to move from here."

From you, she knew he meant, but he had to go and sooner than either of them might want. Ignoring that troubling reality, she leaned her elbow on his chest and smiled. "If we stay here, you won't get to find out what else I had in mind for tonight," she teased.

* * *

Jase offered her a crooked grin, liking this new assertive Nickie, and tapped the tip of her nose playfully. "I'll be up for whatever you want. Just not for a little while."

He was still half-hard inside her and enjoying the feel of her around him and above him. Memorizing every nuance of her to keep with him for when this night was over. That realization stole the last remnants of pleasure, but he forced that worry aside, wanting to focus on the now with all its goodness and of course, with Nickie.

She must have sensed his thoughts since she said, "I'm glad we finally did this, Jase."

He smiled reassuringly and nodded. "I am, too, Nickie. It can only get better from here."

She smoothed her hand across his chest which was still sweaty from their lovemaking and the heat of their bodies pressed together. "It would be nice to cool off, don't you think?" she said and looked toward the ocean.

Early June and the Atlantic would be more than cool. The water would be downright freezing, but as he met her gaze, and noted the brief hot look she gave him, he realized that she had more in mind than just a quick dip.

"Is this something else you've wanted to do – "

"For a very long time. You don't know how many summers I sat there reading – "

"Pretending to read obviously," he kidded and playfully chucked her under her chin.

She chuckled and shook her head. "Yeah, I confess. I can't deny it any more. I was paying more attention to you than to the book."

"I'm honored. I know how much you love to read." He skimmed a finger across the blush of color that came to her cheeks and then trailed it down across her lips. He traced the edge of them with that one finger, over and over.

"Don't get all full of yourself, Jase. I did finally read all those novels," she teased back and kissed the tip of his finger.

"And I'm glad you did," he said. Because he knew their time alone was running short and he was totally game for fulfilling her fantasy, he asked, "So are you ready for that swim?"

She grinned and hopped to her feet. "Last one in has to do what the other one says."

She bolted for the water and he scrambled to his feet and raced after her, not that he'd mind losing. So far he'd liked everything she'd asked of him.

Yeah, I've definitely liked it, he thought as his gaze zeroed in on her perfectly-formed ass as she ran in front of him.

The ocean was smooth as glass tonight and reflected back the bright moon which glittered like diamonds along the surface of the water. Only a few small waves lapped at the shore.

Nickie rushed headlong into the first few feet of water. She turned and faced him, wrapped her arms around herself, and jumped up and down as she shouted, "Shit, Jase. This water is freezing."

Didn't he know it after years of being a lifeguard?

But he also knew there was only one way to get past the cold.

He hurtled toward her and tackled her into the surf, breaking her fall with his body and scooping her up against him as he brought them to the surface.

"Shit, Jase. Shit, that was cruel," she said as she pulled her hair back and shivered in his arms from the cold.

"I warned you it would be cold, babe," he joked and added, "But there is one way to chase away the chill."

She grinned and arched a dark brow. "Just one?"

He laughed out loud, the sound alive in the early morning. He brought his body flush against hers and cupped the ass he'd been admiring just moments before. The tips of her breasts were tight hard points against his chest and he bent and sucked them into his mouth. They were salty from the sea, but that taste left quickly thanks to the sweetness of Nickie's skin.

She wrapped her arms around his head and held him close and the shivers of cold were soon replaced by ripples of desire. Heat built between their bodies at every point of contact.

He urged her to wrap her legs around him and found her center with his one hand, caressing her and building her passion. Playfully nipping at her breast as he said, "I was the last one in. Tell me what you want, Nickie."

"You. All of you, inside me. Now, Jase. Now," she said and he grasped her ass and positioned her for his entry. He drove in with one sharp thrust.

Chapter 7

Nickie cried out at his rough entry and the almost pleasure-pain it brought.

She hadn't realized just how tender she was from their lovemaking, but there was no avoiding that every inch of her body was agonizingly sensitized.

Thankfully he didn't move, but let the gentle ebb and flow of the ocean around them slowly carry them upward until the sensations crested and sent waves and waves of pleasure through their bodies.

He continued to hold her long after and she didn't let go, keeping him tight to her with her arms and legs and kiss after kiss until it was no longer possible to ignore the frigid water and the first blush of an early summer dawn on the horizon.

They hurried back to the blanket where she slipped on her cover-up and he tucked the blanket around them to dry and warm their bodies.

Their hips bumped against each other as they climbed the steps to the boardwalk cutting through the dunes and onto the lawn.

At the edge of the flagstone terrace, she stopped and he faced her, a questioning look on his face.

She cupped his cheeks, rose up on tiptoes and kissed him, her heart swelling and almost bursting at the thought the night was over. That he'd be leaving soon.

"It'll be okay, Nickie," he said and swiped his thumbs across her cheeks and the tears there.

She hadn't even realized she was crying.

With a sniffle and a hesitant smile, she nodded and dropped a quick kiss on his lips. "It'll be okay," she repeated and laced her fingers with his.

As they sauntered across the terrace and into the house, the muted sounds of activity came from the kitchen.

It was probably Rosie, their housekeeper. She raised a finger to her lips, warning Jase to keep silent as they avoided the kitchen, scurried up the steps, and back to her room.

He tossed away the blanket and she shivered again, this time from the cold of the air conditioning on her damp skin.

"I need a hot shower," she said and quickly added, "Will you join me?"

At his doubtful look, she said, "Just a shower, Jase. A quick one to warm up and wash away the salt."

With a quick sexy grin, he said, "Now that's a promise I wish you wouldn't keep."

"Come on." She grabbed hold of his hand and hauled him into her bathroom. She shucked off her cover-up and stood by the immense shower stall to get the hot water running through the multiple shower heads.

"Is this a car wash or a shower?" he teased and nestled behind her, wrapping his arms around her waist as he waited with her.

"Very funny, Jase. You'll thank me when your squeaky clean and deliciously warm."

He chuckled and nipped the crook of her shoulder. "I think I'm already getting warm, Nickie."

"Yeah, I can tell. I guess Marines can always rise to the occasion," she teased since despite his earlier comments, he was gradually hardening against the small of her back.

"Oohrah," he huffed playfully and rubbed his hips against her.

Waving her hand through the water spewing from the shower heads, she was satisfied it was hot enough and opened the stall door. Together they stepped beneath the cascade of water and she turned to face Jase.

"Mmm, that water does feel good. Hot. Wet." His voice was low as he skimmed his erection back and forth across the slick wetness of her belly.

"Amazing thing about water. It's wet," she kidded.

He grinned and her insides twisted at that little boy smile, but even as they did, she had to admit to one little problem. "Jase, I'm a little – "

"Sore? I'm sorry about that, babe. I know this is all probably too much in just one night."

Her heart stuttered painfully and her stomach clenched at his words. She smoothed her hands across his damp shoulders and down his arms to his hands. She twined her fingers with his and said, "Is that all this is or ever will be? Just one night?"

* * *

Jase knew the answer he wanted to give, but didn't yet trust that she was ready for a full out admission of love. Maybe he wasn't ready for it either. Or if he was being totally honest with himself, maybe he wasn't ready in case she decided to reject him.

"That's up to you, Nickie," he said hesitantly.

She met his gaze, hers suddenly clouded and filled with doubt. She worried her lower lip with her teeth and he leaned forward and kissed that spot. Whispered against her lips, "No regrets, remember?"

"No regrets," she whispered back and answered his kiss, opening her mouth to him and accepting his every lick, bite, and taste. Exploring his mouth with hers until he was nearly ready to come just from the pleasure of her kiss.

He held back his release, wanting just a little more of her to remember for when he was gone.

Bending, he caressed her breasts and helped himself to the taste and feel of her delicious tits, smiling against them at her urgent cries of need.

He moved lower, kneeling before her and as his gaze skipped up to hers, there was no doubt about what she wanted.

He parted her gently, mindful of her tenderness. Softly he brushed a kiss across her clit as the warm water streamed down her body and between her legs.

She moaned and shifted against him. She grabbed hold of his shoulders and her nails bit into his skin as she held him tight.

The sharp sting of them made his balls hard and he groaned against her clit from his need.

She gasped his name and urged him up, parting her thighs as she did so. Guiding him to her and he eased in slowly. Carefully. Stood there joined with her as the water rained down on them and against them. Warmed every inch of their bodies that wasn't already heated from their caresses.

He locked his gaze with hers as he braced his hands on the shower stall behind her head. Her long hair was seal black from the wet and plastered against her head and shoulders, exposing her heart-shaped face and long elegant neck. Her expressive hazel eyes were almost cocoa with desire and so alive with everything she was feeling at that moment.

God, but she's beautiful and she's mine, he thought.

She cradled his cheek and skimmed her thumb against his rough morning beard. "Jase," she began hesitantly, but then something came over her. He could see it in her features as she plowed on, all doubt gone.

"I love you, Jase. God, I so love you and if you don't love me back, please don't say another word, 'cause I don't think I could handle it right now."

He dug his fingers through the wet strands of his hair and grinned broadly. "God, Nickie. I love you, too," he said and emotion overwhelmed control.

He came inside her, spilling himself deep within and a moment later, her release exploded around him, milking him. Drawing him ever deeper.

For long moments they stood there, holding onto satisfaction for as long as they could. Forgetting the world around them for as long as they could.

But as his watch alarm beeped in warning, it was impossible for them to face the inevitable.

Their one night together was over.

Chapter 8

Nickie leaned against her door, her arms trapped behind her body to keep her from doing something stupid, like begging him not to leave.

She bit her bottom lip to keep from crying – again – as Jase approached, dressed all in black once more. Leaving her exactly as he'd come to her for their one night together.

Maybe not exactly. She didn't think that either of them could ever be the same again after tonight.

He paused in front of her and started to speak, but then his normally mobile and smiling lips snapped closed and into a harsh thin line.

She understood.

What other words could they possibly say to each other? What words could possibly make any difference in what they both knew had to happen that morning?

She inched higher on her tiptoes and kissed him, a hard and urgent kiss that she hoped communicated all that she was feeling.

When they broke apart, she sniffled back her tears, scrubbed her face with shaky hands, and offered him a watery smile. She didn't outright cry, but she couldn't speak past the tightness in her throat and was thankful that he remained silent as well.

With a quick, almost curt nod, and another hard urgent kiss, he rushed out the door, leaving her behind to deal with the emotions swirling around in her brain. Emotions she didn't have time to fully explore because she knew that she had to be downstairs soon for the big bye-bye breakfast that her parents had planned for the Hart family.

Only she wasn't sure she was ready to say goodbye. Not when she'd confessed her love to the man of her dreams. The man of her fantasies who had turned out to be so much more than she ever could have imagined.

She hurried to the bathroom and splashed cold water on her face to keep away another bout of tears. She had no energy or desire to do much with her hair, so with a hurried brushing and a few quick twists she put it up in a messy top knot.

Ignoring the quick glance of the pale strained face of the woman in the mirror, she rushed back into her bedroom.

She grabbed the suitcase where she'd carted home her clothes for the weekend, snatched a pair of faded low-rise jeans and panties from it, and put them on. Without much care, she grabbed a bra and a pale blue and white baby doll t-shirt that Tommy had gotten her at the university store just before graduation.

Fortifying herself with a deep inhalation, she hurried from her room and down to the kitchen. She breezed over to where Rosie was working at the large island peninsula in the middle of the room. Hugging the plump woman who was almost like a second mom, she asked, "Is everyone down for breakfast already?"

"Everyone's down and you're dad is giving Jason a very determined glare. He seems to think Jason is the reason you're not at the table yet," Rosie said and glanced back over her shoulder and toward the dining room.

She plucked a ripe strawberry from the plate Rosie was preparing and earned a lighthearted slap on the hand. "Can't you wait until you're sitting down at the table like everyone else?"

Nickie craned her neck and peered through the doorway to the dining table where her family and Jase's was gathered and where her chair next to her dad sat conspicuously absent.

"Why would my dad think that Jase is the reason I'm not there yet?" she asked, dragging a sharp chuckle from Rosie. Her laugh was followed by her hushed whisper as Rosie leaned close and said, "Your dad was up early and came down to make himself some coffee just as I arrived."

Which meant that he might have seen her and Jase sneaking in from the beach.

"Shit," she muttered.

"Yes, I think that's what he said when he saw you and Jason heading up the stairs together."

Rosie put the finishing touches on the large platter of fruit salad and eyed her, the glance thoughtful and surprisingly supportive. "It's time to face the music, Nickie."

Yeah, it was, but she hoped the music didn't turn out to be a funeral dirge.

She followed Rosie into the dining room, a bright smile on her face, not that she was feeling all that happy. She hugged her dad, mom, Tommy, and Jase's parents before taking her spot at the table at the empty chair beside her dad. The spot beside her was normally reserved for her brother, but he was sitting next to their mom and Jase's mom. As she met his gaze, hers questioning, he winked and then shot a quick glance at Jase, who was sitting in Tommy's normal spot.

"You're late," her father said, a combination of anger and annoyance dripping from every word.

"I'm sorry, dad, but I couldn't sleep last night," she said and avoided looking at Jase, although as she sat, he placed a comforting hand on her thigh. His actions were hidden from view by the table.

"Funny thing, but I had trouble sleeping as well," he said and glared at the two of them, but said nothing else as Rosie stepped between them to place the fruit platter on the table.

Her family had never been big on formalities, especially not with the Harts who had shared so many good times with them.

"Well, I'm starving," Tommy said and grabbed the spoon from the fruit platter to serve himself.

"Dig in," her mother urged and whatever her father might have wanted to say was forestalled by the exchange of plates from one hand to the other as people served themselves from the pastries, bagels, eggs, bacon, and fruit that Rosie had prepared for the meal.

She wasn't very hungry. Her stomach was twisted up like a pretzel as each second ticked by and became one second closer to the time Jase would leave with his parents. But she also knew her father and eagle-eyed mother would know something was up if she didn't eat.

She'd always had a healthy appetite and breakfast was her absolutely favorite meal. There was no way she'd skipped it unless some major shit was going down.

She loaded her plate with eggs, bacon, a bagel and some of the fresh fruit, and forced herself to start eating.

"Would you like some coffee?" Jase asked and offered to pour from the carafe in his hand.

"I'd love some, thanks," she replied, maybe a little too formally. Anyone watching them would hopefully never believe that they'd spent the entire night fucking each other's brains out, but as she grabbed the carafe from him, their fingers brushed and a salvo of desire and heat exploded through her body.

With a shaky hand, she poured coffee for her dad, managing to spill a good amount into his saucer.

"Are you sure you haven't had too much coffee already, Nickie? You seem kind of jittery," her father said and steadied her hand with his.

"Not enough, actually." When she finished pouring and set the carafe on the table, she fixed her coffee with a few spoonfuls of sugar and cream and took a big swallow. "Heaven," she said and ignored her brother's snicker.

"Heaven is Rosie's French toast," her brother said and then called out to the housekeeper, "How come you didn't make your world famous French toast, Rosie?"

Rosie came in a second later with a plate heaped with blueberry walnut pancakes which she took right to Jason. With a wry grin at Tommy, she said, "Because these are Jase's favorites and I wanted to make something special for him before he left."

She dropped her fork at Rosie's words, but Jase's reassuring touch on her thigh provided the strength for her to pick it up and try to act as if everything was normal.

Only it wasn't.

The man of her dreams was sitting beside her and he'd be gone in a few short hours. After that, who knew how long it would be before he would be back home, only home wasn't New Jersey anymore. Not since his parents had moved away months earlier.

She grabbed her coffee cup again and took a bracing swallow, hoping the heat of the coffee would help warm the chill that had suddenly seized her heart.

It didn't.

Somehow she managed to eat, not that she was hungry. Especially not as her dad decided to pile on with the reason for this special meal. He raised his juice glass and said, "To Jason on his commission and deployment. We hope you come home soon, as well as safe and sound."

"Thank you, sir," he said respectfully and lifted his coffee cup to clink it against those being offered by everyone except her. She somehow couldn't muster the strength to raise her cup at first, but then managed a hasty tap against his to avoid scrutiny.

The rest of the meal passed in relative silence as everyone ate. Every now and then someone would ask Jase a question about his assignment and she listened intently, trying to picture how the time would pass. What he'd be doing. What she'd be doing. How long it might be until they were together again.

"So you're not set to ship out until next weekend? You have this whole week off?" Tommy asked Jase while gazing at her directly.

"I have the week off, but there are some things I promised my parents I'd do this week," he said and forked up a big mouthful of pancakes.

"Jase and I have work to do on the new house," his dad chimed in.

"And we haven't really seen him all that much since we moved down to North Carolina," his mom added and looked at her son with love and pride.

"Right," Jase said around the mouthful of food, but squeezed her thigh beneath the table as if to say, "I'm sorry. I'd rather be with you."

But he couldn't be with her. In that second, though, it came to her what she had to do.

It was something that was illogical and so not like her.

It would risk her heart even more than she already had by giving him his one night.

But it was the right thing to do.

She laced her fingers with his and brought their joined hands to rest on the table in full view.

Everyone's attention zoomed to that spot, including Jase's, as she said, "Would you mind very much if I went with you? I'm off from school and even if I get the summer intern position, I don't have to start until next month. So I'm free to go and I'd like to spend some more time with Jase."

Her dad's dark bushy eyebrows shot up high, looking like two crow's wings about to take flight on his forehead. Her mom brought a shaky hand to her mouth and her eyes watered. Tommy grinned from ear to ear, obviously pleased and let out a loud "Oohrah."

Jase's parents were obviously surprised, but smiling in approval.

"Are you serious, Nicole? Do you know what that means?" her father asked, but his voice lacked the bluster and upset she had expected.

She glanced at Jase and her gaze lovingly swept across his face. She smiled and said without any doubt, "I know what it means, Dad. I love Jase. I want to be with him."

* * *

In his wildest dreams, Jase had never expected this. Never imagined Nickie would truly commit for more than the one night much less surprise everyone like this.

But she had and he wasn't about to doubt why or how. He was going to go big and then go home with her.

"And I love, Nickie, Mr. and Mrs. de Silva. I have for a while," he said and looked directly at her father, knowing that he'd appreciate that he had no hesitation in making the declaration.

Her father slapped his hands on the table dramatically and said, "Well, it's about time. We all kept on wondering when the two of you would finally come to your senses."

"All?" Jase asked and examined the faces of the family members gathered around the table and Rosie, who had rushed in at the loud sound of Nickie's father's hands hitting the wood. It was evident that each one of them agreed with the statement, but even more importantly, they all were clearly happy with the outcome.

"It was obvious, dude," Tommy said, laughter ringing from his voice.

Nickie squeezed his hand and with an equal dash of humor said, "Obvious to everyone but the two of us. I guess we're kind of dense."

He grinned as he looked at her. "Yeah, I guess we are. It's a good thing we finally did something about it. Any regrets, Nickie?"

Her smile was brilliant and unrestrained. "No regrets."

That was all he needed to here.

He leaned over and kissed her, sealing their unspoken promise with that kiss. Grinning against her lips with joy.

When they broke apart, she said, "I have to go pack."

"I'll help," he said and they excused themselves from the table and headed to her room. Once inside, he wrapped his arms around her waist and drew her near. He asked her once again, just in case. "Are you sure about this, Nickie? About us?"

She nodded and cradled his cheek, offering up that beaming smile again. "I've never been more sure of anything in my life, Jase."

She broke away from him and walked to the small overnighter sitting on the floor by her bed. He joined her and briefly examined the suitcase. "That doesn't look like it'll hold much."

With a sexy grin, she said, "I don't think I'll be needing all that many clothes."

"No, I don't think you will," he said and kissed her again, grateful that their one night had brought the promise of many many more nights together.

* * *

From the Author: I hope you enjoyed Nickie and Jase's story. I loved the sexiness and playfulness they could share with each another and of course, giving them their happily-ever-after. One big reason for that happy ending was Nickie's brother Tommy and his urging Jase "to go big or go home."

I can't wait to find the perfect match for Tommy and give him a very special night as well. Look for ONE SPECIAL NIGHT, Tommy's story, later this year.

❦ THE END ❦

About the Author

Caridad Pineiro is a New York Times and USA Today bestselling author and RITA® Finalist. Caridad wrote her first novel in the fifth grade when her teacher assigned a project – to write a book for a class lending library. Bitten by the writing bug, Caridad continued with her passion for the written word and in 1999, Caridad's first novel was released. Over a decade later, Caridad is the author of nearly 40 published novels and novellas. When not writing, Caridad is a wife, and mother to an aspiring writer and fashionista. For more information, please visit www.caridad.com or rebornvampirenovels.com.

Follow Charity on Twitter at https://twitter.com/caridadpineiro and on Facebook at https://www.facebook.com/Caridad.Author.

Additional Books by the Author Writing as Charity Pineiro

NOW AND ALWAYS June 2013 ISBN 1490362770
FAITH IN YOU July 2013 ISBN 1490412697
TORI GOT LUCKY December 2013 ISBN 1494775182
THE PERFECT MIX March 2014 1495948234
TO CATCH HER MAN April 2013 ASIN B00JJ7RK1C

Additional Books by the Author Writing as Caridad Pineiro

Books in The Gambling for Love Romantic Suspense Series

THE PRINCE'S GAMBLE November 2012 ISBN 9781622668007 Entangled Publishing
TO CATCH A PRINCESS August 2013 ISBN 9781622661329 Entangled Publishing

Books in The Sin Hunter Paranormal Romance Series

THE CLAIMED May 2012 ISBN 978-0446584609 Forever Grand Central Publishing
THE LOST August 2011 ISBN 978-0446584616 Forever Grand Central Publishing

Books in The Sins Paranormal Romance Series

STRONGER THAN SIN November 2010 ISBN 0446543845 Forever Grand Central Publishing
SINS OF THE FLESH November 2009 ISBN 0446543837 Forever Grand Central Publishing

Other Novels by Caridad

THE FIFTH KINDOM July 2011 ISBN 9781426891885 Carina Press
SOLDIER'S SECRET CHILD Dec 2008 ISBN 0373276109 Silhouette Romantic Suspense

Novellas

GHOST OF A CHANCE, paranormal short story November 2012 ISBN B00AUGV89G Caridad Pineiro Publishing
HER VAMPIRE LOVER October 2012 ISBN 9781459242289 Nocturne Cravings Novella
NIGHT OF THE COUGAR June 2012 ISBN 9781459231153 Nocturne Cravings Novella
THE VAMPIRE'S CONSORT April 2012 ISBN 9781459222731 Harlequin Nocturne Cravings Novella
NOCTURNAL WHISPERS February 2012 ISBN 9781459221437 Harlequin Nocturne Cravings Novella
AMAZON AWAKENING December 2011 ISBN 9781459282766 Available Harlequin Nocturne Cravings Novella
WHEN HERALD ANGELS SING novella in A VAMPIRE FOR CHRISTMAS October 2011 ISBN 0373776446 HQN
AZTEC GOLD January 2011 ISBN 9781426891045 Carina Press Novella
Crazy for the Cat in MOON FEVER Oct 2007 ISBN 1416514902 Pocket Books

Books in THE CALLING/THE REBORN Vampire Novel Series

VAMPIRE REBORN, March 2014, ASIN B00J3GHA3C
DIE FOR LOVE, December 2013, ASIN B00H6EFD5U Entangled Publishing
BORN TO LOVE, November 2013, ISBN 9781622663705 Entangled Publishing
TO LOVE OR SERVE, October 2013, ISBN 9781622663477Entangled Publishing
FOR LOVE OR VENGEANCE September 2013 ISBN 9781622662937 Entangled Publishing
KISSED BY A VAMPIRE (formerly ARDOR CALLS) October 2012 ISBN 9780373885589 Harlequin Nocturne
AWAKENING THE BEAST Collection featuring HONOR CALLS October 2009 ISBN 0373250940 Silhouette Nocturne
FURY CALLS March 2009 ISBN 0373618077 Silhouette Nocturne
HONOR CALLS February 2009 ISBN 9781426828362 Nocturne Bite
HOLIDAY WITH A VAMPIRE December 2007 ISBN 0373617763 Silhouette Nocturne

THE CALLING COMPLETE COLLECTION October 2008 ISBN 9781426807657 Silhouette Includes Darkness Calls, Danger Calls, Temptation Calls, Death Calls, Devotion Calls, and Blood Calls–as well as a the online read Desire Calls.
BLOOD CALLS May 2007 ISBN 0373617631 Silhouette Nocturne
DEVOTION CALLS January 2007 ISBN 0373617550 Silhouette Nocturne
DEATH CALLS Dec 2006 ISBN 0373617534 Silhouette Nocturne
TEMPTATION CALLS Oct 2005 ISBN 0373274602 Silhouette Intimate Moments
DANGER CALLS June 2005 ISBN 0373274416 Silhouette Intimate Moments
DARKNESS CALLS Mar 2004 ISBN 0373273533 Silhouette Intimate Moments

Romantic Suspense Series

SECRET AGENT REUNION Aug 2007 ISBN 0373275463 Silhouette Romantic Suspense
MORE THAN A MISSION Aug 2006 ISBN 037327498X Silhouette Intimate Moments

Made in the USA
Middletown, DE
13 June 2022